Mirror, Mirror

Garfield's Apprentices

LEON GARFIELD

Mirror, Mirror

illustrated by
ANTONY MAITLAND

HEINEMANN
London

William Heinemann Ltd
15 Queen Street, Mayfair, London W1X 8BE

LONDON   MELBOURNE   TORONTO
JOHANNESBURG   AUCKLAND

To Jane

First published 1976
© Leon Garfield 1976
Illustrations © Antony Maitland 1976

434 94031 3

Printed and bound in Great Britain by
Morrison & Gibb Ltd., London and Edinburgh

Between Glass House Yard and Shoemaker's Row lies Friers Street, where Mr Paris's premises occupies a commanding position on a corner In the gloom of the November evening his shop window flares out extravagantly, as platoons of candles execute various dancing manoeuvres in flawless unison. On closer inspection, however, they turn out to be a single candle reflected in a cunning display of looking-glasses. Mr Paris is a master carver of mirror-frames; golden boys and golden grapes cluster round the silver mirrors and seem to invite, with dimpled arms outstretched, the passer-by to pause and contemplate himself.

Inside, in the dining parlour, the family are sitting down to supper: Mr and Mrs Paris—a handsome couple who will be middle-aged when it suits them—Miss Lucinda, their young daughter, and Nightingale, the new apprentice.

Nightingale has not long arrived. He has scarcely had time to wash himself before sitting down to table. All day he has been tramping the streets with his father, a Hertfordshire joiner, and gaping at the multitudinous sights of the town. All in all, it has been a solemn day, what with the many unspoken leave-takings between father and son, the looks over the tops of toasting tankards of ale, the deep pressings of hands, the sentences begun and left half finished as the same melancholy thought strikes them both . . .

They have never before been parted; or at least, not for more than a day. But now the inevitable time has come. Ten pounds has been paid for the apprenticeship and Daniel Nightingale is to embark alone on the great voyage of life . . . as the village parson had been pleased to put it. Like all such voyages, it is to be seven years long, and the only provisions that the father might properly give his son to take with him have been the wise precepts he himself has treasured up and written down from his own seven years of apprenticeship.

Never come between your master and mistress . . .

Nightingale looks up at the table at Mr Paris and then down the table at Mrs Paris; the husband and wife gaze at one another with identical smiles, as if each is the reflection of the other's heart.

Carry no tales or gossip between master and mistress, nor chatter with the servants of their private affairs . . .

A greasy girl comes in with a dish of mutton and a carving knife. She puts them both on the table with a glance at Nightingale that makes his blood run cold.

Look upon your master as another parent to you . . .

6

Nightingale catches Mr Paris's eye, but finds it altogether too slippery to hold. Mournfully he remembers his own parent; only a few hours ago he was "Daniel, boy . . . Dan, dear . . ." Now that fond distinction has been shorn away and he is plain 'Nightingale'.

Perhaps now that I'm just a Nightingale, he thinks as a plate is set before him, I ought to sing for my supper? He smiles to himself, not having thought of many jokes before, wit in Hertfordshire being as thin on the ground as turnips are thick. Mr and Mrs Paris continue with their own smiles and the table presents an amiable aspect . . . with the exception of Miss Lucinda, the master's pretty daughter. She dislikes the new apprentice for no better reason than that he has failed to recognize her as the queen of the household. She knows it is every apprentice's ambition to wed his master's daughter and she cannot endure the notion of being a rung in someone else's ladder to the sky. She is not much beyond fourteen, with fair hair, fair skin and a general brilliancy about her that suggests she has caught some shining complaint from her father's wares.

"I hope and trust, Master Nightingale," says Mr Paris, never taking his eyes off his wife, "that at the end of your seven years we will all be as contented and smiling as we are now?"

The apprentice, caught with his mouth full, nods politely. At the same time, mournful thoughts of the day return. Seven years; seven long years . . .

After the meal, Mr Paris rises and shows Nightingale where he is to sleep. According to usage, the apprentice's bed is made up under the counter in the front room that serves as showroom and shop; thus if dreams come, they are more likely than not to be dreams arising from the day's work, so no time will be wasted. Mr Paris bids Nightingale goodnight and leaves him with a wax candle which he must be sparing with, as it is to last him for a week.

The apprentice mumbles his thanks and, when he is alone, prepares to say his nightly prayers. He is scarcely on his knees before the door opens abruptly and startles him. His master's daughter stands in the doorway. He has no time to observe her before she calls out:

"Nightingale! Catch!"

She tosses something towards him that glitters in the candlelight like a speeding star. The apprentice is too surprised to do more than put out a hand that just touches the object before it falls with a crash to the ground. It is, or, rather, was, a looking-glass. Now it lies on the floor, shattered into silver knives and slices. Miss Lucinda smiles.

"You've broken a mirror, Nightingale. That means seven years' bad luck."

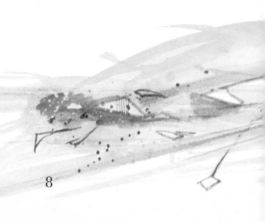

"You slept well, lad?"

Mr Paris, smooth and glazed looking from his morning shave, came into the shop. The apprentice—hours of work, six until eight—had already taken down the shutters and swept the floor. Ordinarily as clear and truthful as daylight, Nightingale remembered his father's precept—*carry no tales* . . . He nodded in answer to his master's inquiry and said nothing of the sleepless night he had spent, caused by Miss Lucinda's grim prophecy of an apprenticeship that was to consist of seven years' solid bad luck.

He took breakfast with the family while the morning sun streamed into the parlour, enveloping Miss Lucinda and making her hard to look at. At half past seven he went to the workroom where Mr Paris's journeyman—an ancient craftsman with the head of a prophet and hands like the roots of trees—was already at work.

"Job," said Mr Paris. "This is Nightingale."

The journeyman looked up from his carving and smiled at the new apprentice. Everyone in the household seemed to smile . . . excepting the daughter. Nightingale, with the natural confidence of a good-looking youth, felt that sooner or later he would be able to melt her. His heart began to beat more easily.

"Come here, Nightingale," said Mr Paris. "Tell me what you see."

The master drew a cloth from a handsome mirror that stood upon an easel as if it had been a painting.

"Look closely. Take your time, and tell me what you see."

The apprentice, doing his best to reflect his master's

smile, obeyed and looked in the mirror. A soft, blushing face that required shaving but once a week, beamed awkwardly back at him.

"Why, me, sir!"

"Indeed?"

Nightingale's heart sank as he heard Mr Paris's voice take on a decided edge. What *should* he have said? He felt as if he was suddenly standing upon nothing.

"Is it not very vain of you to think, Master Nightingale, that I should keep an image of you in my workroom? Why should I do such a thing? Who would buy it?"

The ancient journeyman sniggered; Nightingale went as red as a radish.

"Job," said the master. "Tell him what *you* see."

Job, still sniggering, presented his own splendid countenance to the glass.

"I see vines, Mister Paris; and the fruits thereof. I sees naked little boys, what might be angels, a-buttressing the mitres. And at the bottom, finely 'graved, I see 'Josiah Paris, Mirror Frame Carver. Friers Street. Blackfriars.' "

"In a word, Nightingale," said Mr Paris, "he sees a *frame*. A well carved frame. He does not see his own image, my lad."

The journeyman smirked and went back to his carving, while Nightingale felt that his seven years' bad luck had begun with a bull's eye.

"In our line of trade," went on Mr Paris, covering up the mirror, "a craftsman—be he master, journeyman or apprentice—looks *at* a mirror, not *in* one."

"Yes, sir. I see, sir."

"A mirror," said Mr Paris, expanding his thoughts and person at one and the same time, "is nothing."

"Yes, sir."

"And yet it is everything. It is like life itself; it gives back only what is put into it. Smile—and you create a smile; scowl and you double the distress."

"Yes, sir . . . I see that now, sir."

"Human life is a mirror," mused Mr Paris, as if his ideas were being reflected off mirrors inside his head. "Thus the idle apprentice who gives his master only a tenth of his time, gets back, from life, only a tenth of its value."

"Yes, sir. I'll always remember that."

"There's much wisdom to be gained from mirrors and the framing of them, Nightingale. It is not for nothing that we say, when a man thinks deeply, he *reflects*."

"He always does that," chuckled the journeyman when the master had gone. "It were the same with the last 'prentice and the one afore him."

"Where are they now?" asked the third apprentice, sweeping woodshavings industriously. "Didn't they stay out their seven years?"

The journeyman's chuckle faded into a remote smile and he bent over his work.

"It ain't for me to say. Carry no tales is a good rule for journeymen as well as 'prentices."

Soon after nine o'clock, the shop bell jumped and Nightingale was summoned to assist his master. A tall, well-spoken gentleman had called to purchase a looking-glass for his wife. Books of patterns were duly consulted and several samples fetched out for demonstration of their quality. To Nightingale's surprise, the gentleman, who'd been overbearing to begin with, turned soft as putty and easy to please. Although he'd been as awkward as the devil about the patterns, the mirrors themselves had quite the opposite effect. He fixed on a simple oval and made his escape as soon as price and delivery were settled.

Nightingale opened the door and bowed him out and into his carriage.

"Consumed with vanity," said Mr Paris, handing his apprentice the pattern books and glasses to put away. "That gentleman was eaten up with vanity. You saw how he couldn't bear to look closely at the mirrors? Only a vain man avoids his reflection so very particularly. He has such a fixed notion of his countenance that he will admit nothing that might disturb it. You saw what an ugly hooked nose he had? Most likely, inside his head, that nose was aristocratic. He had a hairy mole above his lip. Most likely he thinks of it as a rare ornament."

Nightingale nodded in a bemused fashion and caught himself wondering if the radiant Miss Lucinda looked much in mirrors, and if she did was it a mark of modesty or was she contrary to all philosophy?

They dined at one: the journeyman in the workroom and Nightingale sitting down with the family after he had helped the greasy girl to bring out the dishes from the kitchen.

"I don't ordinarily take on a lad with an irregular cast of feature," said Mr Paris, smiling down the table. The apprentice felt his cheeks grow warm, and he tried to absorb himself in the plate before him.

"Nor have you done so this time," said Mrs Paris, glancing at Nightingale before smiling back at her husband. "You really couldn't say he was wanting in countenance."

The apprentice, though grateful for the compliment, felt his cheeks grow hotter; and Miss Lucinda's eyes seemed to be scraping the skin off his bones.

"In our line of trade," said Mr Paris to the household in general, "a dropped eye, a marred cheek, bad teeth or a bent nose are highly disadvantageous. The possessor of such a countenance would not be welcomed in this establishment. Bodily misfortunes we can tolerate, providing they are not exposed. Job has a fallen hip, and, I'm told, swollen knees. For my part, I've no objection to a wooden leg, even; if the stump be kept wholesome and clean. But the face must be as Caesar's wife—" Here he acknowledged Mrs Paris with a peculiarly fine smile; "—the face must be above suspicion. We must be able to look in mirrors without awkwardness, without shame. A man with a defect of countenance, in such circumstances, might fall into a melancholia and go mad of it. In our line we must be able to endure and endure ourselves with equanimity. I don't say, with pleasure, but with equanimity. It cannot have escaped your notice, Nightingale, that we are a particularly fine-looking family?"

The apprentice looked up and saw his master's daughter sitting on her father's right hand. With every intention of being agreeable, he began to study her features with admiration and zeal. A look of sharp spite rippled across her face as if it had been a reflection in water, suddenly shuffled by a wind.

At eight o'clock the old journeyman took his day's wages and carried his magnificent head limpingly on his fallen hip and swollen knees out into the November dark. As he left, the old man asked the apprentice if he would care to join him for a glass of ale nearby? Reluctantly, Nightingale declined; he was weary to the point of faintness from his sleepless night and he ached for his bed.

He stumbled through the evening meal in a dull silence and afterward begged to be excused from sitting with the family in the parlour. He was given permission to retire but not without a warning that his candle was to last out the week.

Thankfully he went into the shop and had scarcely taken off his coat when, as on the previous night, his door flew open.

"Nightingale!"

It was Miss Lucinda. Nightingale flinched in the expectation of something else being tossed for him to catch. This time, however, she had come on another errand.

"I want you to come and look at a mirror of mine," she said remotely. "It's upstairs, in my parlour. Come and look at it."

The apprentice, swaying beside his bed as if he would fall asleep before falling down, said: "Yes, Miss Lucinda."

He believed that he must have made some inroads in her affections and that this was her way of showing it. He followed her upstairs, hoisting himself by the banister rails and counting them to keep awake. She led him into her little room where, in imitation of her father's workroom, there was an easel on which stood a shrouded mirror.

"I want you to look in the mirror, Nightingale, and tell me what you see."

He was to be tested again. He tried to think. What should he say this time? Should he praise the frame? Or, if she herself was reflected in the glass, should he praise her? What would please her most? Much depended on his words . . .

He stood before the mirror, preparing himself . . .

She snatched the cloth away. Nightingale shrieked aloud.
A black-socketed skull grinned back at him! He trembled
violently, believing, for a moment, that he'd seen an un-
canny portent of his own doom. Then he perceived that
he'd looked, not in a mirror, but through clear glass behind
which had been arranged the death's head.

17

Miss Lucinda laughed—and he rushed from the room in terror. Downstairs he lay on his bed, sobbing bitterly on account of the fright he'd had, on account of being the object of a hatred he could not understand, and on account of being parted from those who loved him. He felt he could never sleep again . . .

Next morning he awoke suddenly. Someone wild and amazed was staring him in the face. He leaped from his bed —to discover that a mirror had been set to confront him. He fancied he heard a sound of laughter in the passage outside.

He got through the day in a fog of bewilderment and unhappiness. The shop bell rang and rang; customers came and went; he bowed them in ʿnd bowed them out; he swept and tidied and stood stock still whenever Mr Paris chose to unburden himself of more wisdom than Nightingale thought ever should have been contained in a mortal head; and whenever he was alone, he crouched down behind the counter, held his aching head in both hands and wept like a child.

"I saw you crying behind the counter," said Miss Lucinda, as she passed him in the passage. "And all the street saw you, too."

Filled with a new dismay, he ran back into the shop. High over the counter a mirror had been tilted so that everything was reflected outwards. He climbed up on a chair and took it down carefully, trying to avoid seeing the fear in his own face. After that he was cautious about every expression and every action; he could never know for certain whether he was being reflected, and watched.

Was it possible that the master knew what his daughter was doing? Perhaps he'd instructed her? Perhaps this was all his testing time? Perhaps it was like those ancient trials by fire and water to temper the spirit and make it worthy? Only his was a trial by mirrors . . .? "A craftsman must endure and endure . . ." he murmured to himself as he sat, absorbed in such fanciful reflections, in the little necessary-house at the end of the yard. He had gone there more to relieve his mind than his body; and indeed, as his thoughts drifted, he did come to a kind of melancholy peace.

He raised his eyes as if to heaven; a shaft of light was shining through the ventilating aperture above the door. It fell upon a tilted square of silvered glass. Miss Lucinda's face was gazing down with a look of disgust and contempt. He cried out—and she vanished. He heard her jump down from whatever she'd been standing on; then he heard her feet pattering away.

He pulled up his breeches and hurried back into the workroom, feeling guilty and ashamed of being alive. He picked up a broom and began to sweep the shavings from round the feet of the ancient journeyman; then he went to fetch Job's beer.

The old man was working on a design of oak leaves and children's faces; patiently he tapped away with his mallet so that the bent gouge he gripped inquired into the wood like another finger. From time to time he laid his tools aside and set the frame against the mirror it was being carved for . . . and his marvellous prophet's head gazed back with a remote and dreamy rapture.

"Your beer, Mister Job, sir."

19

The journeyman nodded. "Lay it on the bench, Master Nightingale."

The apprentice obeyed and looked again over Job's shoulder at the unfinished frame. The children's faces were sharply defined and were all exactly alike. They were Miss Lucinda . . .

Nightingale wondered if he dared question the journeyman about their master's daughter? He longed to ask the old man what *he* thought of her. Did she ever speak to him? Did she ever speak to anyone? Even her father and mother never seemed honoured with a word from her; nor, for that matter, did they speak much to her. Was she, perhaps, not their child? Or was she a mad child, suffered to roam the house and never checked for fear of provoking something worse than tricks with mirrors? Surely Job would know what she was?

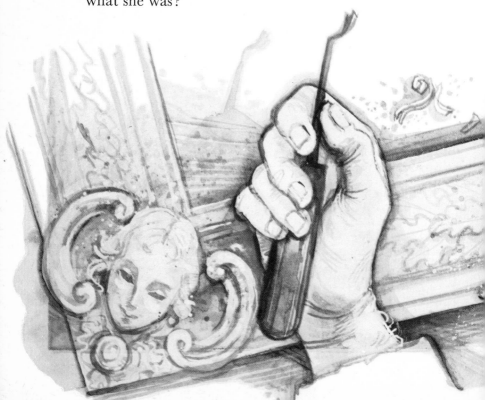

The journeyman, without taking his eyes from the mirror, reached for his beer.

"Recognize 'em, Master Nightingale?"

"They're Miss Lucinda, ain't they, Mister Job, sir?"

"And a good likeness, don't you think? They was to have been angels. That's what they are in the pattern book. But I thought Miss Lucinda would be a nice fancy. It'll please the master. And that's what you and me's here for, Master Nightingale. Journeymen and apprentices alike must always please their master. Just as you aim to please your own pa at home."

So she's an angel, thought Nightingale; and found himself left with no choice but to keep at his work and show, by all means in his power, that his chief aim in life was indeed to please his master.

After all, when he came to think about it all carefully, he wasn't so badly off. No one had clouted him; no one had injured him bodily. . . . "Country born and country bred," he muttered with rueful philosophy. "Strong in the arm and weak in the head. And what's wrong with that? Well, not weak, exactly, but good and solid. Nothing too fanciful. When all's said and done, there's no sense in thinking and thinking about something a country body can't hope to understand. And—and they say worse things happen at sea. So I ought to be thankful I've not been sent for a sailor! Besides, who knows but Miss Lucinda will come to respect me for holding my tongue about her tricks? Who knows, but I'll turn out the industrious apprentice yet and wed my master's daughter? They say it does happen . . ."

He pursued this line of comfort, with varying success, for the remainder of the day; whenever he passed Miss Lucinda he endeavoured to express in his smile, forgiveness for her cruelty and admiration for her beauty at one and the same time. On such occasions, she did not seem to see him. Then—

"Nightingale!"

Once more she was at his door and again demanding that he should come and look in her mirror. He sighed, and steeled himself for another look at the death's head. As he followed her he even prepared some sort of philosophical remark that he hoped would impress her with his worth.

"Look at yourself, Nightingale," she said. "Look at what you are." She took away the cloth. A pig's head, still bloody from the butcher's axe, peered back at the apprentice.

He tried to laugh; but in truth he felt too sick and

frightened to do more than imitate the grin of yesterday's skull. He stumbled out of the room and made his way back to his bed.

On the next day he came upon mirrors laid in different places; mirrors that caused him to fall headlong down a pair of steps outside the workroom, that led him to gash his forehead against an open door, that made him trip over a piece of wood that wasn't there and so to break a costly jug.

There was no mirror any more in the privy, nor was there one above the counter; but that didn't help. He couldn't be easy in his mind that they really weren't there. Indeed, he could not be easy in his mind about anything . . .

He found himself walking about the ill-lit house like one newly blinded—with hands outstretched, never knowing whether he was coming to a reality or its reflection. His chief hope was for the night; it was only in darkness that he could feel secure and be able to distort his face with weeping and anguish without restraint. Until that blessed time, he did what he could to wear the glazed smile of his master, his mistress and Job, the lame old prophet in the workroom.

When night did come, he was too sick and giddy in his brain to do more than nod when Miss Lucinda, like a white spirit, came to summon him to her mirror again. Wearily he climbed the stairs to the pretty little parlour. A dead rat. He shrank away. Truly had the country Nightingale flown into a forest of glass and thorn.

In the blackness of his bed he cried out against his father's ambition that had sent him forth on so dreadful a journey.

"I want you to be better than I am, Daniel," he had said aspiringly. "I want you to be something more than a humble joiner. You shall be a master carver and, God willing, one day you will be carving cathedral pews and screens and all manner of beautiful things. That's what I want for my son."

"And who knows," mused his mother, "but that some day, like your father before you, you will wed your master's daughter? It's the dream of every apprentice, you know; and the reward for the industrious ones."

"We are making a great sacrifice," said his father.

"But no sacrifice can be too great," said his mother, kissing him. "Always remember that."

Lying in a sea of tears, Nightingale remembered; and feeling his mother's kiss, wondered whether he himself was the sacrifice that could not be too great?

He knew there had been two other apprentices before him. Had they suffered as he was suffering? Had she hated them, too? This possibility gave him a crumb of comfort, and he fell to supposing they'd fled, no matter what the consequences, even though rebellion in an apprentice was reckoned a great sin. He tried to smile. Most likely they'd been town sparrows and knew better ways of the world than did a country Nightingale.

"I think you should know, Nightingale," said Mr Paris, over the evening meal, "that we are pleased with you." As usual, he smiled down the table at his smiling wife, while on his right hand sat Miss Lucinda, the devil-angel of the household. "I am writing to your father to tell him that we find you courteous and respectful."

Nightingale smiled fixedly down at his plate. A week had passed and his spirit was broken as surely as the looking-glass he'd dropped on his first day.

He longed to cry out, to protest against the monstrous injustice to which he was being subjected. Every shame, every piece of spiteful humiliation that could be inflicted by mirrors had been daily visited on him; and nightly he'd been condemned to go to bed with an image of himself in a mirror that was no mirror, as something hateful and below contempt.

"Look at yourself! Look at yourself! Look at yourself!"
Miss Lucinda commanded, standing in her pretty, blue-papered parlour, and uncovering, one after another, the framed sights of worms, a hanged man's head, a broken piss-pot with "Nightingale" scrawled on it in black . . .

"I can tell you now, Nightingale," went on Mr Paris, cheerfully, "that when I brought you out of Hertfordshire, I had my doubts about country lads. One hears such tales of boys new to the town running after all manner of gaudy nonsense; worshipping the golden calf, one might say. An apprentice, my boy, must put his master above everything else. It's the only way to get through his seven years with honour and profit."

Nightingale said, "Yes, sir," and went out to fetch his master another jug of ale.

"Look at yourself, Nightingale. Look in my mirror. See what you are tonight."

Miss Lucinda stood in her parlour, while the apprentice, already without his jacket—for she'd come to him late—swayed before the shrouded easel. Dully he'd been wracking his brains to imagine what she'd concealed this time behind the false glass? What hideous object could she have scavenged this time to frighten him with and to show him what he was?

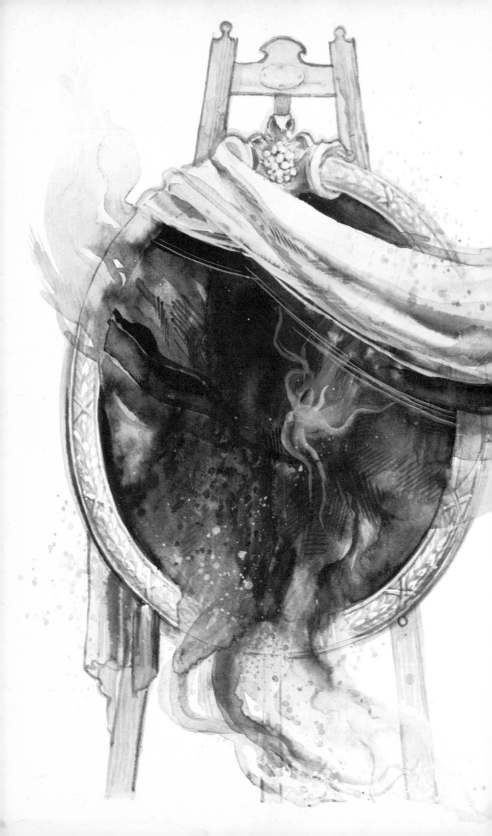

"Look, Nightingale!"

She took away the cloth. The apprentice felt his head spin and his ears roar. Framed in the glass that faced him was—nothingness. Blackness, a bottomless pit . . .

The extreme shock of meeting with such utter emptiness overbalanced him. He felt himself begin to fall forwards, as if he was actually being sucked into the hole before his eyes. A black velvet bag had been placed behind the glass . . .

"Nothing," she said. "That's what you are now. Nothing . . . nothing."

What would he be tomorrow, he wondered, as he half fell down the stairs? What was there on the other side of nothing?

It was a damp, misty morning with a cemetery chill on it; Job, who was afflicted with rheumatism in addition to his other bodily misfortunes, asked if the apprentice might be sent to Greening's in Glass House Yard to fetch a mirror that was cut and waiting? It would have been a cruel torment if he'd had to walk there himself.

"Nightingale?"

"Yes, Mister Paris, sir?"

"Can you find your way to Greening's in the Yard?"

"Yes, sir. Directly, sir."

"Nightingale!"

"Yes, sir?"

"Check the glass carefully. They'll pass off rubbish if they can. No flaws, mind; no cracks in the silver, no spots of tarnish round the edges."

"Yes, sir."

"How will you judge, Nightingale?"

"I—I'll look at it . . . all over."

"And what will you see, Nightingale? Yourself. Much good that will do us, eh, Job?"

The old man rubbed his knees and sniggered.

"The human countenance, Master Nightingale, is no yardstick for perfection; not even yours. Words, lad; that's what's needful. *In the beginning there was the Word*, and all that. Here, take this—"

He gave the abashed apprentice a card on which was

printed, bold and black, something that might have been Hebrew for all Nightingale could tell.

"Just you hold it up to the glass they give you and read the letters clean and clear. Then you'll be able to see what's what."

Nightingale put on his coat, took the card and set off. The very idea of going out after his distressful week revived him considerably; he felt, as he shut the shop door behind him that he was emerging from a peculiarly bad dream. However, once outside, this comfortable sensation was reversed by the mistiness of the morning that had the effect of rendering the buildings and street indistinct and much more dreamlike than the house he'd just left. Consequently he was quite unable to throw off the creeping uneasiness of what he might be shown that night in Miss Lucinda's mirror. What was that could lie on the further side of nothing?

He walked quickly, without particularly meaning to; the chill in the air forced him to be brisk and vigorous, even though he felt, as they say, distinctly under the weather. He reached Glass House Yard and found Greening's without difficulty.

It turned out to be more of a warehouse than a shop, with tall racks in which white-covered mirrors were stacked like huge, wordless volumes in a library for giants. The air in the beamed and boarded interior was brooding and pensive . . .

"Mirror for Mister Paris," said Nightingale to a short, weaselish apprentice who appeared reluctantly from the obscure shadows at the back of the shop.

"Mirror for Paris!" shouted out the weaselish one to the shadows he'd just left.

"Third shelf along on the right. Got his name on it!" came a shout in reply.

The mirror, wrapped in white muslin, was brought down and laid on the counter.

"Sixpence on the clorf," said the weasel, hopefully.

"I heard that!" came the shout from the back. "There's nothing to pay and well you know it!"

The weasel shrugged his thin shoulders.

"Got to try and make ends meet," he said amiably.

Nightingale smiled. The apprentice's attempt at sharp practice had been transparent enough even for Nightingale to see through. The other, not at all abashed, beamed over the counter.

"Givin' you a 'ard time, I see."

"What do you mean?" asked Nightingale, uneasily.

"Paris and that 'orrible bitch of a daughter of 'is."

"No such thing!" Nightingale shrank in terror from the temptation of pouring out his misery to a stranger. He smiled again, this time with the glazed smile that was the livery of his master's house.

"You look fair worn to the bone," said the weasel, with interest.

"Stop gossiping and give him the mirror!" shouted the invisible one.

"Ain't gossiping. Just offerin' comfort to a fellow 'prentice in distress. It's Paris's new one."

There came a thunder of large feet on bare boards and Mr Greening himself issued from the cavernous depths of

his shop. It was not to be wondered at that he kept in the shadows; he was extraordinarily ugly with a monstrous nose that was afflicted with warts, like an old potato. He pushed his apprentice aside and laid his grey and silver stained hands on the counter.

"You always look as pale as a corpse, son?" he inquired, studying Mr Paris's new apprentice with small, bright eyes that resembled chips of glass.

"It must be the weather, sir," said Nightingale, with a pang of alarm.

"How long have you been with Mr Paris?"

"Only a week, sir."

"God help us!"

"I—I'm quite happy there, sir . . ."

"As the dying man said when the last drop of feeling left him," remarked Mr Greening. "Well, well, you'd best take the glass and be off."

Eager to escape, Nightingale took hold of the wrapped mirror.

"Aren't you going to check it?"

Nightingale blushed and remembered the card. He produced it; Mr Greening nodded approvingly, unwrapped the mirror and obligingly held it up. Nightingale presented the card to the glass's silver face. The black words leaped out at him:

FOR NOW WE SEE THROUGH A GLASS DARKLY; BUT THEN FACE TO FACE: NOW I KNOW IN PART: BUT THEN SHALL I KNOW EVEN AS ALSO I AM KNOWN.

Mr Greening put the mirror down.

"All right, son?"

Nightingale nodded, but found himself staring into the air where the mirror had been. The words seemed to remain suspended in nothingness before him. He felt quite dizzy with trying to read them.

"Here!" he heard Mr Greening say. "Fetch him some brandy and water. And mind—I know just how much brandy's left! Mirrors," he went on kindly, reaching out a hand to guide Nightingale to a chair, "can sometimes unsettle the strongest stomachs."

Nightingale sat down. He couldn't imagine what had come over him. He felt faint and sick. He put it down to the strong smell of polishing oil that suddenly seemed to be everywhere. Gratefully he drank off the brandy and water —which contained less water than might have been expected on account of the apprentice being generous with his master's property—and rose to go. His legs had gone like water . . .

"Sit still for a while. Wouldn't do to go dropping that mirror on your way back. Seven years' bad luck, you know . . ."

Nightingale nodded and shuddered; he looked up at Mr Greening whose nose now seemed so enormous that it filled Nightingale's world. The warts were like large, bald mountains and the tufts of hair that sprouted from the nostrils were like the forests of the night. Way, way above this fleshy landscape gleamed Mr Greening's eyes, as distant as the stars . . .

"I'm going to be sick," said Nightingale.

"Got a bucket here," said the weasel.

"Broke a mirror," confessed Nightingale, after he'd brought up his breakfast, "on me first day. That's what done it."

"That's what done it."

"She threw it to me," said Nightingale, after a pause. "And that's when it all started."

"What started?"

"Things."

"What things?"

"Mirrors . . . mirrors . . ."

"He's crying," said the weasel, brightly.

"Mustn't carry tales," remembered Nightingale; and hiccuped.

"Won't tell a soul," said Mr Greening sombrely. "What about the mirrors?"

"Everywhere. Even in the privy. And the one upstairs.

35

That's the worst . . ."

"Won't tell a soul," said Mr Greening again. "Why is it worst?"

So Nightingale told him . . .

What with the smoking of countless chimneys and, in particular, the dirty guffaws of the furnaces in Glass House Yard, the mist had condensed into a fog. Mr Paris's apprentice, emerging from Greening's, had immediately been plunged into the November breath of the town, which smelled as if all the inhabitants had belched after partaking of the same bad dinner.

He was carrying, in addition to the mirror he had been sent for, a wrapped box of about the same size as the mirror but some six inches deeper. It was heavy and seemed to grow the more so as he walked. However, the weight of it under his arm was as nothing compared with the weight on his heart.

He had betrayed his sacred trust. How he'd come to pour out all the details of his wretchedness to the ugly Mr Greening, he would never know. He believed that, somehow, he'd dozed off and talked in his sleep. He looked back towards the strange shop as if for an answer; but the establishment was already lost in the fog. He had a sudden idea of throwing the heavy box away; he did not know what it contained and he was deeply afraid of it.

"It's a sort of mirror, you might say," the weaselish apprentice had said, and grinned malevolently.

Mr Greening had warned him not to look in it himself. Under no circumstances was he to open it until she, and she alone, stood before it. He was to set it upon an easel, in a good light, and bid her look. The weasel had laughed aloud, and even Mr Greening had smiled as if in terrible anticipation.

"What is it? What will it do?" Nightingale had asked, trembling with shame over his betrayal and fear for the consequence of it.

For answer, Mr Greening had rubbed his grotesque nose and recalled the words on Nightingale's card.

"Then shall you know even as also you are known," he'd said, and left it at that.

If the early morning had been dreamlike, the day had

now grown up into nightmare; Nightingale wouldn't have been surprised if he'd awakened with a start to find himself under the counter in Mr Paris's shop. In the past he'd had dreams every scrap as convincing . . .

A fire came looping at him out of the thick air.

"Light you home, mister?"

The fog had brought out the link-boys with their torches like a plague of fireflies. Nightingale jumped, and stared at the thin, pale child who stood before him, holding aloft a flaming length of tow that really served no better purpose than to draw attention to the evil state of the weather. The light reached no further than a yard before it came back off the fog and bathed the link-boy in its glow.

"How much?" asked Nightingale.

"'pends how far," said the link-boy, blinking away tears brought on by his flaming pitch.

"Friers Street. Mr Paris's shop."

"'s only round the corner. Off Shoemaker's Row. Cost you a penny."

Nightingale closed with the offer and the link-boy set off, miraculously weaving his way through a nothing that hid countless bulky somethings. Dazedly Nightingale kept his eyes on the streaming fire that superfluously added its own smoke to the atmosphere. He wished he'd got rid of the box before the link-boy had appeared.

"Nothing like a bit of fire for keeping out the cold," said the link-boy, and offered Nightingale a warm.

Although the torch shed no useful radiance in any particular direction, there was no doubt that Nightingale found its presence a comfort.

"Friers Street," said the link-boy suddenly, and waited while his customer searched and found a penny. Then, payment being made, he flickered off and was rapidly extinguished in the premature night.

"And where have you been, Nightingale?" asks Mr Paris severely.

"I come over all queer at Mr Greening's," says Nightingale humbly; and means it with all his heart. He has managed to deposit the mysterious box under the counter without being seen, before presenting himself to his master.

Mr Paris looks closely, then resumes his glazed smile. He believes his apprentice, having satisfied himself that he certainly *looks* queer.

"He was taken over queer at Greening's," he tells Mrs Paris as they sit down to table.

Nightingale looks up from his plate apologetically—and sees Miss Lucinda staring at him in triumph. He tries, with his eyes alone, to make some sort of approach to her; but without the smallest success.

For the rest of the day he is given only light tasks; Mr Paris is not an unkindly man, when things are brought face to face with him; he is really concerned for his pale, listless-looking apprentice. He begins to wonder if he has been altogether wise in caging a country Nightingale . . .?

Nightingale himself has similar thoughts; he dreads more than ever the coming of the night. Try as he might, he cannot imagine what terrible vengeance on his behalf has been concealed in the box. What if his master's daughter should be killed by it? That would turn him into a murderer!

The ugly Mr Greening and his weaselish apprentice haunt his mind like a pair of malicious spirits in a darkened room. He resolves he will do nothing with the box. He is quite set on that; he'll not raise a finger to provide either the light or the easel . . . Then, quite out of the blue, Mr Paris bids him carry the easel from the workroom into the shop, ready to display Job's frame which will soon be finished.

Nightingale's heart falters as fate comes in on Mr Greening's side.

"Candle in the window won't do us much good on a night like this," says Mr Paris, looking out into the deplorable weather. He glances back at his distinctly frightened and ill-looking apprentice, and then at the gloomy counter under which he is to sleep. "But keep it going all the same. Leave the shutters down and let a little brightness inside for a change, Nightingale."

Thoughtfully he turns the looking-glasses in the window so that they face inwards and reflect the candle quite strongly upon the empty easel in the shop.

Nightingale feels a sense of panic concerning the powers of Mr Greening as he watches the father unknowingly arranging matters conveniently for the striking down of his own daughter.

At last the apprentice is left alone. He fetches out the box, takes off its outer coverings and places it on the easel. There is only a thin lid between him and whatever the box contains. He has determined that he will look in it himself. The candlelight, multiplied by the looking-glasses, dances and glitters on the box. Nightingale reaches out a hand, trembling in every limb at what he is about to behold. Mr Greening and his apprentice rise up before his inner eye and scream warnings . . .

"Nightingale!"

It is *she*. She has opened the door and stands just within the room. Her eyes fall upon the easel and the covered object upon it. She sees the apprentice standing before it, pale as death.

"What have you got there?"

Nightingale withdraws the hand that had been about to uncover Mr Greening's gift.

"A—a sort of mirror, you might say," he answers, helplessly repeating the words of the weaselish apprentice. To his horror, he hears, in his own voice, a reflection of the weasel's mocking tone.

Miss Lucinda hears it, too.

"Let me see it," she says, and pushes him to one side.

He smiles in a dazed, glazed fashion, feeling that it is fate that has pushed him and not Miss Lucinda. She reaches out, but seeing his smile, hesitates.

"You've arranged this, haven't you?"

He does not answer; he does not need to.

"It's your revenge, isn't it?"

"Not mine," mutters Nightingale, thinking of the ugly Mr Greening.

"You've put something vile in there," says Miss Lucinda, contemptuously. "Some disgusting thing out of your own brain."

She lowers her hand and Nightingale sighs with audible relief. She falls silent and Nightingale hangs his head in an effort to avoid her brilliant and penetrating eyes. Then he looks up and sees that once more she has raised her hand and now rests it upon the thin lid of the box.

"Your thoughts," she says. "They're here, aren't they? What do they amount to? A toad? A piece of filth? Something dead and rotting? Something so foul and degrading that it's best covered up? Let's see, Nightingale, once and for all, how mean and depraved an apprentice's mind and heart can be!"

She laughs, and before Nightingale can stop her, she lifts up the lid. Light streams into the box, and the lid falls with a clatter from her hand. Nightingale turns away in terror. He waits for some shriek or sound of death; but there is only silence. Fearfully he looks back. She has not moved. A terrible pallor has spread over her face; even her lips, for all their redness, have gone a greyish white. What horrible, deadly thing did Mr Greening hide in the box?

She breathes deeply as if suffering from an intolerable constriction; and the something so degrading that it should have been covered up, gazes back at her. Helplessly she looks, with pitiless clarity, upon—herself.

Mr Greening's box contains no more than a perfect mirror. Neither ripple, tarnish nor flaw interposes to alleviate the girl from the image that she herself has so monstrously described.

Her expression, halted by shock, has remained unchanged from the look she'd worn before. Every mark of scorn, contempt, lamed ambition and cruelty are bloodlessly plain. The very smile of deep pride—that had once lent her a sort of distinction—robbed of its colour, has become a dull sneer. The eyes, fixed on the bland surface of the glass, have lost all brightness, all penetration, and become as glass; glass eyes in a glass head . . .

Filled with guilt and fear, Nightingale approaches to see what it is she has seen. As he moves, she gives a low and anguished cry, which resembles, not so much a sound as a shudder made audible, for it is accompanied by a continuous, violent trembling.

She is mortally afraid that he will see what she has seen, that he will see her as she now sees herself. His countenance joins her as she watches it, examines it minutely with ever-increasing agony.

"But it's only glass!" says Nightingale, with gentle amazement.

"Only glass," she repeats, finding in the apprentice's face nothing worse than relief and bewilderment. "Quicksilver, lead and glass . . ."

"That's how they make mirrors, isn't it?" says Nightingale, as if persuading a child out of too strong a dream.

"They put lead, as thin as paper, on the glass and pour quicksilver over it," she murmurs. "I've watched it being

46

done. My father once took me. I'll take you, if you like . . .
some day . . . if you like . . ."

Nightingale moves closer. He cannot really help himself.
. . . For a moment, their faces are reflected together, then
their joined breath mists the glass, obscures them and
dissolves eyes, lips, cheeks and tears into a strange, double
countenance, seen, as it were, in a glass brightly.

But the candlelight, reflecting busily off all the looking-
glasses from the window, keeps catching at the corners of
Nightingale's eyes so that he seems to be looking into the
heart of a diamond.

He blinks and turns away, glancing, as he does so, from
mirror to mirror, in each of which he sees his master's
daughter. Sometimes he sees her in profile, sometimes just
the coils of her golden hair, sometimes the curve of her
cheek and the projecting edge of her lashes; and sometimes,
as strange as the other side of the moon, her second profile.

. . . He looks and looks, and as far as his eyes can see, his universe is filled with Lucindas . . .

And she, at last abandoning her reflection to the eyes of another, follows his example and roams the angled mirrors. Everywhere she sees him, but cannot, by reason of the confused architecture of light, make out for certain what it is he is gazing at. She looks and looks, and as far as her eyes can see, her universe is filled with Nightingales . . . and their song is suddenly sweet.

Outside, the fog piles up and rolls comfortably past the window of Mr Paris's shop; from somewhere in the invisible street, a gentleman curses as he trips over a lamplighter's ladder, and from every darkened corner come the link-boys' eager cries of:

"Light you home, mister! Light you home, ma'am!"